Tiny Troll Treasury

The Enchanted Frog

Illustrated by
Joe Veno

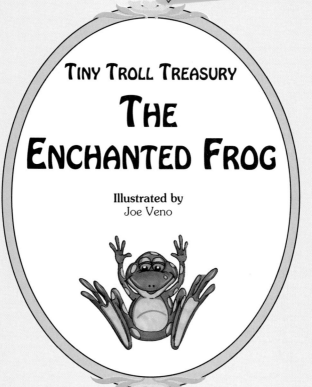

Publications International, Ltd.

Once upon a time, a little troll princess was playing with her golden ball in the garden. She tossed it into the air again and again.

All of a sudden, a gust of wind blew the golden ball away from the princess. The ball fell into the garden well instead of into the princess's hands.

"What shall I do?" cried the princess. "My favorite ball is lost forever in the deep, dark well!"

A strange voice croaked, "I can help you."

The princess turned and saw a frog watching her from a sunny spot in the garden. "Can you really bring my golden ball back to me?" she asked.

"I will bring back your golden ball, but you will have to pay my price," said the frog.

"I will pay anything! I promise!" said the princess happily.

The frog jumped into the deep, dark well. Down, down, down he went. The princess heard a distant splash and wondered what price the frog would have her pay for the return of her golden ball. Would he ask for gold or silver or diamonds?

It was not long before the frog climbed to the edge of the well. He was tired and wet, but he held the golden ball out to the princess.

The princess ran to the frog and grabbed the ball from his green hands. She did not remember her promise to the frog, and did not even thank him for his hard work.

That evening, there came a knock on the castle door. The king excused himself to see who was there. When he returned, he brought the frog with him.

"Daughter," he said, "is it true this noble frog saved your golden ball from the well today?"

The princess said that it was, and that it was also true that she had promised to pay the frog's price for his favor.

"Frog," said the king, "please name the price that the princess must pay and you shall have it."

"I wish to be the princess's constant companion," said the frog. "I will eat meals with her, play in the garden with her, and sleep at the foot of her bed at night."

At first, the princess was very unhappy, but she knew she would only make her father angry if she did not do as the frog wished.

So from then on, the frog went everywhere and did everything with the princess. They played together in the garden. They ate their meals side by side. The frog, who was quite intelligent, even helped the princess with her lessons.

Many months passed. One day the frog asked, "Do you still hate me because I am a frog, princess?"

"Oh, no, dear frog. In fact, I have grown to love you," she smiled.

"Do you not think I am ugly?" asked the frog.

"I think you are the handsomest frog I have ever seen," said the princess.

The frog lowered his head and asked, "May I have a kiss to prove that you love me? If you say yes, I shall stay with you forever. But if you say no, I will go away and never bother you again."

The princess wondered how she could ever have been so mean to the frog so many months ago. "Of course you may have a kiss," she said.

She closed her eyes and gave the frog a gentle kiss.

When the princess opened her eyes, the frog was gone. Standing in front of her was a handsome troll prince! "Who are you? Where is my frog?" she exclaimed.

"I am your frog," said the prince. "I was under a spell that could only be broken by a kiss from a princess who loves me."

The princess and the prince were married that very day and lived happily ever after.